ARTIST TRANSCRIPTIONS TRUMPET

THE Chet Baker COLLECTION

DISCOGRAPHY

Au Privave, There Will Never Be Another You – Out of Nowhere - CD: Milestone MCD-9191

Cherokee – LP: Prestige 7460 (Groovin' with the Chet Baker Quintet); CD: Prestige 24173 (Stairway to the Stars)

Do It the Hard Way – It Could Happen to You – LP: Riverside RLP 1120; CD: OJCCD-303

Early Morning Mood – New Blue Horns – CD: OJC-087 (Chet)

Freeway – The Gerry Mulligan Quartet - LP: Pacific Jazz 1 (10"); CD – Blue Note 89292

Have You Met Miss Jones? – LP: Prestige 7449 (Smokin' with the Chet Baker Quintet); CD: Prestige 24172 (Lonely Star)

How Deep Is the Ocean – This Is Always – CD: Steeplechase SCCD 31168

How High the Moon, September Song – Chet – LP: Riverside 1135; CD: OJCCP-087

I Get Along Without You Very Well, Let's Get Lost, My Funny Valentine, My Old Flame – Chet Baker Sings – LP: Pacific Jazz 1222; CD: Blue Note 92932

Loaded, Witch Doctor - Witch Doctor - LP: Contemporary C-7649; CD: OJCCD-609

Moonlight Becomes You – The Trumpet Artistry of Chet Baker – LP: Pacific Jazz 1206; CD: 89292

Out of Nowhere – Out of Nowhere – CD: Milestone 9191

Pent Up House, Tune Up – Chet Baker in Milan – LP: Jazzland 18; CD: OJCCP-370

Solar – Chet Baker in New York – LP: Riverside RLP 1119; CD: OJCCP-207

Stella By Starlight – Jazz in Ann Arbor – LP: Pacific Jazz 1203; CD: Blue Note 92932

The Touch of Your Lips – The Touch of Your Lips – CD: Steeplechase SCCD 31122

You Better Go Now – Chet Baker and Strings – LP: Columbia CL 549; CD: Legacy 65562

Photo courtesy of Institute of Jazz Studies

ISBN 978-0-7935-9938-7

HAL•LEONARD CORPORATION

7777 W. BLUEMOUND RD. P.O. BOX 13819 MILWAUKEE, WI 53213

Visit Hal Leonard Online at
www.halleonard.com

Chet Baker

BIOGRAPHY

Chet Baker was one of the most controversial figures in jazz. Self-taught, a musician who could only read a bit and did not know traditional harmony, his performances as a trumpet player, flugelhorn player and singer were often mesmerizing.

He had a small range of about 2 1/2 octaves on his horn, but he contended, "I can say everything I have to say." Baker always had problems with his teeth, which affected his embouchure, and in later years he wore dentures. Because of his various addictions, he often did not show up for concerts or recording sessions. Most American listeners had forgotten him by the 1980s. But Chet continued to play and record in Europe, and on many nights, a performance by Chet Baker was a rich, unique experience.

Chesney Henry Baker Jr. was born on December 23, 1929. His father was an amateur guitarist who played western swing music on local radio. The family moved to Glendale, California when Chet was ten, and at the age of eleven, his father bought a trumpet for him from a local pawnshop. Chet taught himself by listening to the radio and records and playing along, relying on his ear. At about this time, he was hit on the mouth with a rock at school, losing his upper left front tooth. This limited his range and volume, and forced him to alter his embouchure. Hating school, and wanting to get away from his family, he joined the army at the age of sixteen, where he was assigned to an army band in Berlin. During his stint in the service, Chet heard Dizzy Gillespie over Armed Forces Radio, which changed his life.

In 1948, back home in California, Chet enrolled at El Camino College in Los Angeles to take theory and harmony classes, but soon dropped out to attend jam sessions. But he re-enlisted to play in the Sixth Army Band in San Francisco. When he was re-assigned to another band at a fort in the middle of the Arizona desert, he went AWOL; a month later he reported back to San Francisco and was soon given a general discharge.

Returning to LA, he played in more jam sessions, and landed a gig with Charlie Parker at the Tiffany Club in May of 1952. Upon returning to New York Parker told trumpet players, "There's a little white cat on the coast who's gonna eat you up."

Saxophonist/arranger Gerry Mulligan had established residence in Los Angeles, and was arranging for bands and playing at jam sessions. At a Monday evening jam session at a club called the Haig, Mulligan met Baker, liked his playing, and invited him to join a quintet he was forming. One week at the Haig, the featured performer, vibist Red Norvo, asked that the piano be put in storage to give his trio more room on the stand. Mulligan's group rehearsed without the piano, liked the results, and the group remained piano-less. Recordings on the new Pacific Jazz label followed, and the Mulligan group's popularity skyrocketed, becoming the resident band playing the small, eighty-five seat club for six months. The Haig was packed every night, with many celebrities in attendance to hear the 'new thing' in jazz. The telepathy between Mulligan and Baker was uncanny; this quartet is regarded as one of the great legendary small groups in the history of jazz.

However, it was not to last. Baker was arrested for smoking marijuana in December of 1952, the first of many arrests. Mulligan was also arrested for drug possession in June, 1953, and was sentenced to a California prison for three months. Baker hired pianist Russ Freeman as a replacement. Recordings with the new line-up established Baker as a poll-winning leader. Mulligan and Baker would later re-unite for an occasional recording or concert.

Baker made his first vocal recordings in October of 1953. Critical reaction was mixed, but he usually sang at least one number per set from that time on. His playing, singing and movie star looks made him one of the most well known personalities in show business. He appeared in the movie *Hell's Horizon* in 1955, and word in Hollywood was that he was being groomed as the next James Dean. But a European tour that same year was surrounded by tragedy: the death of pianist Dick Twardzik.

Back in the states in 1956, he formed a new group with saxophonist Phil Urso. In 1959, he moved to New York and made several albums for the Riverside label. But he was arrested again for possession of drugs; he was in jail for four months, and his New York cabaret card was taken from him. He decided to move to Italy with his wife and son. In 1960 he was again arrested for drug possession and sentenced to seven years in jail. He only served sixteen months, and was soon playing and recording again. In 1964, he returned to the U.S.; he was now playing flugelhorn because of his continuing problems with his teeth. Work was scarce in New York, so he moved to Los Angeles with his family, which now included two more children.

In July of 1966, while playing a gig in San Francisco, Baker was brutally beaten. He continued to play until, in 1968, he decided to have his remaining teeth pulled and wore a denture for the rest of his life. Forced to re-learn how to play the trumpet, he disappeared for four years to get himself together.

When he started playing again, he found more opportunities for his talent in Europe, and it would be his home base until his death. He had no fixed address and traveled from gig to gig, recording prolifically. Unreliable, often in poor physical shape, Baker missed as many concerts as he played. And yet he was respected in Europe and commanded high prices for concerts and recordings.

In 1987, a fashion photographer named Bruce Weber shot interview and concert footage of Baker, interspersed with interviews of his family and friends. *Let's Get Lost* was first shown in 1988 in Venice; it was later nominated for an Academy Award for Best Documentary.

Baker was busier than ever when he checked into a motel room one evening in Holland. Apparently he had taken both heroin and cocaine, and tried to open a window in the room, falling into the street below. He died in the early morning of May 13, 1988.

AU PRIVAVE

By CHARLIE PARKER

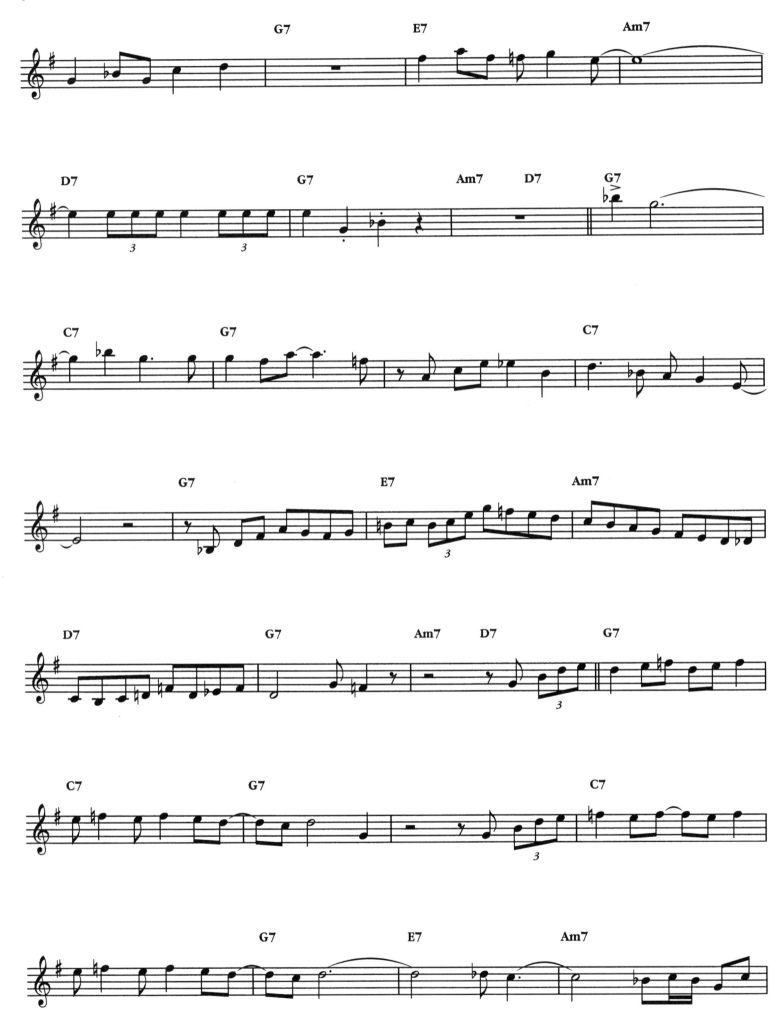

8

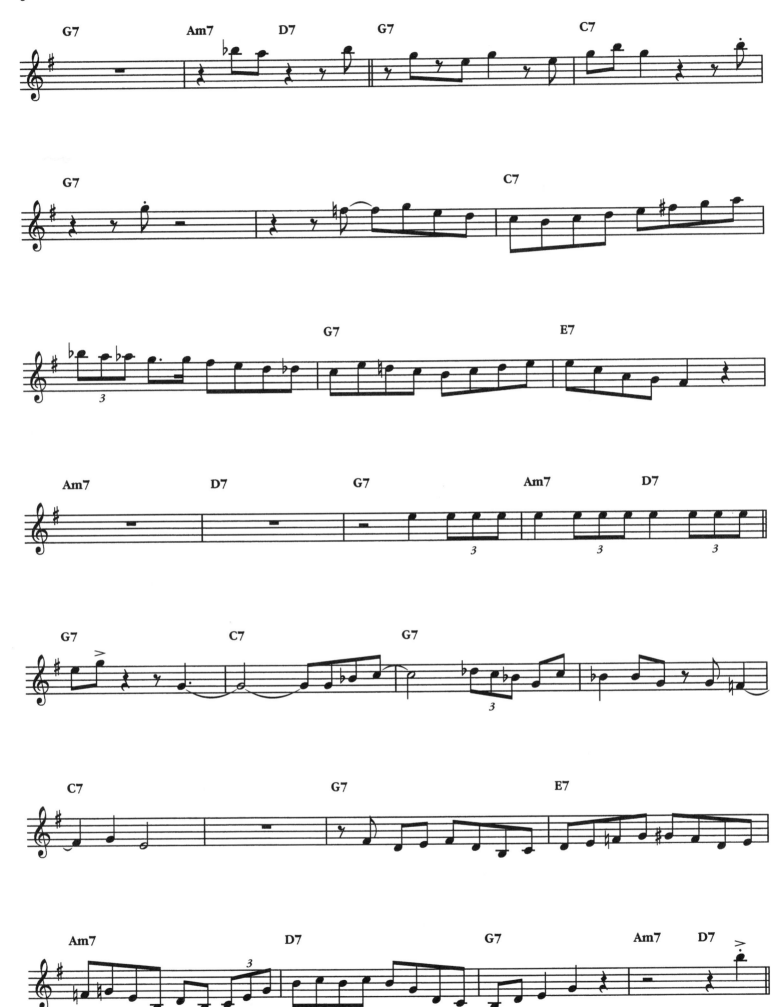

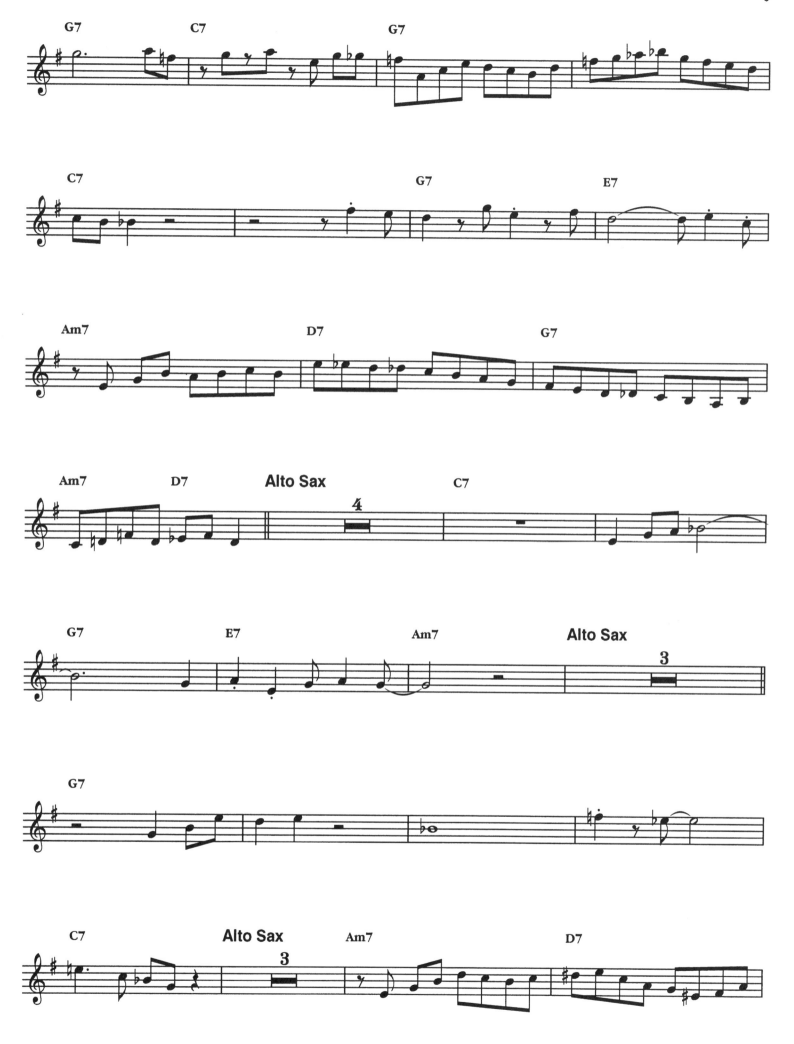

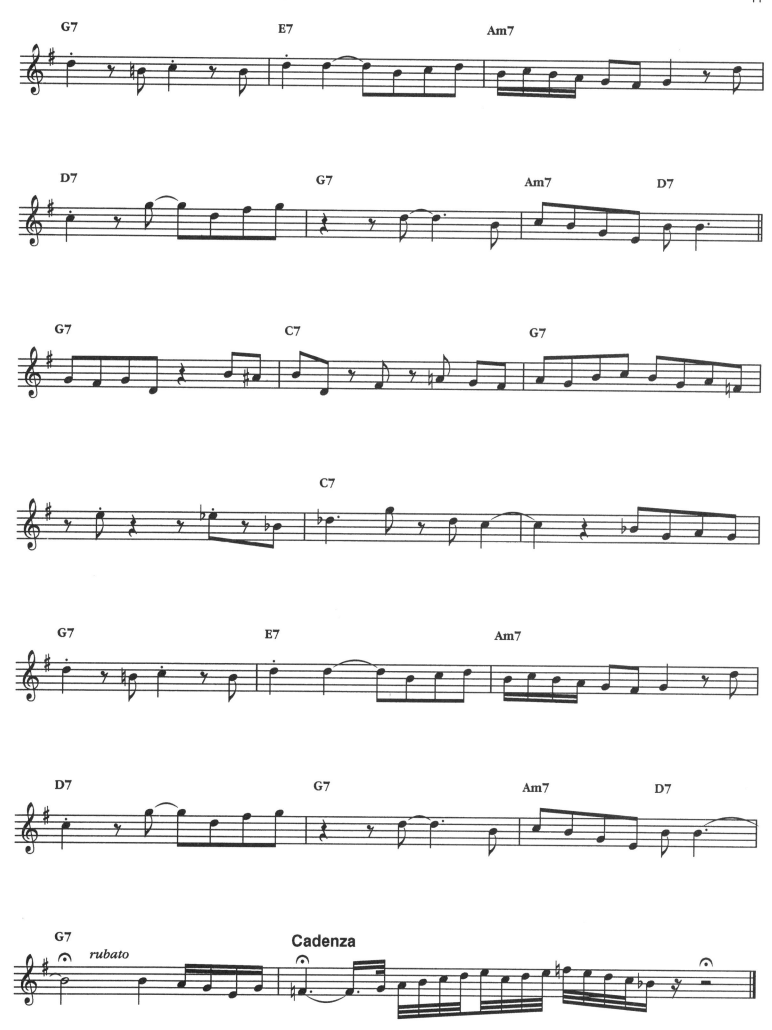

CHEROKEE
(INDIAN LOVE SONG)

Words and Music by RAY NOBLE

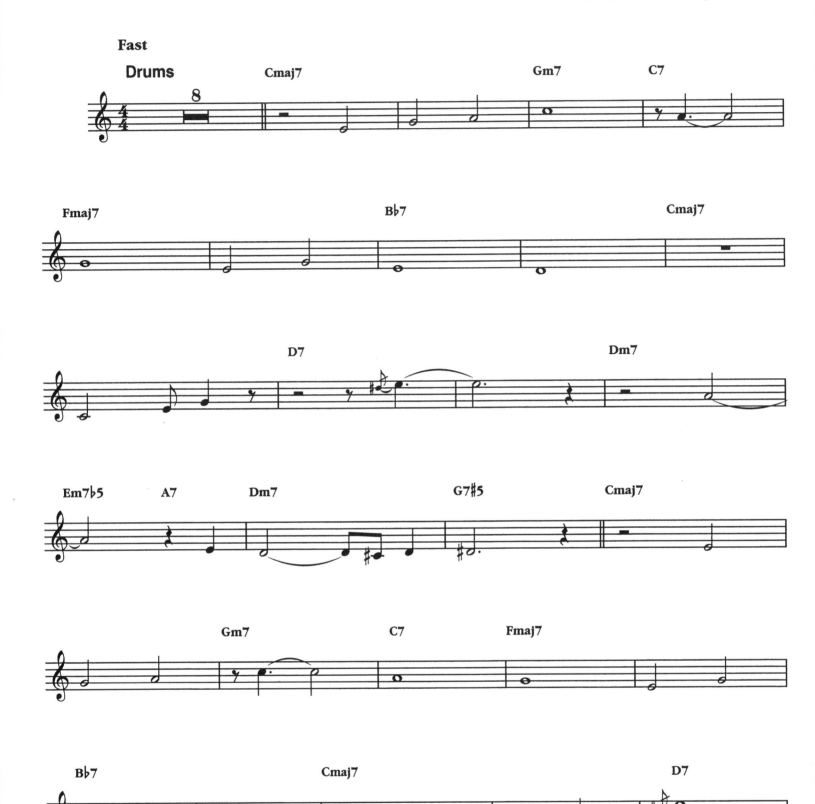

14

16

DO IT THE HARD WAY

from PAL JOEY

Words by LORENZ HART
Music by RICHARD RODGERS

Slowly and quietly

Piano Solo

Do it the hard way and it's ea - sy sail - ing.

Do it the hard way and it's hard to lose;

on - ly the soft way has a chance of fail - ing;

you have to choose.

I tried the hard way when I tried to

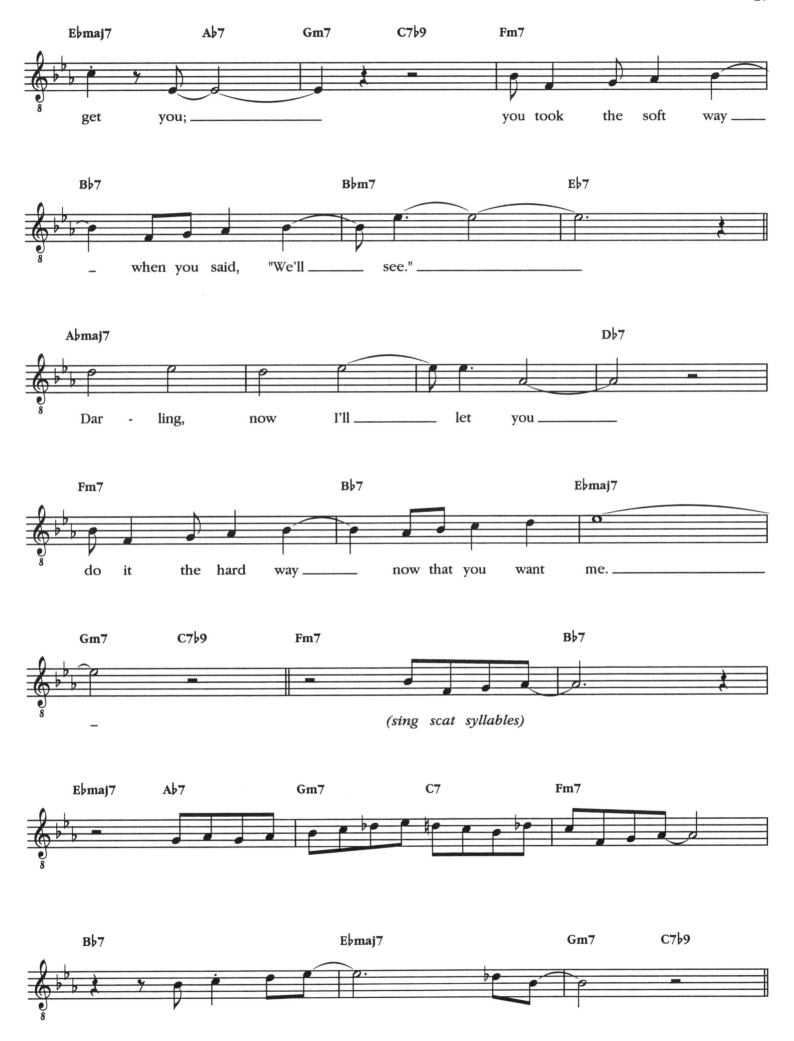

Piano Solo

31

I tried the hard way _____ when I tried to get you; _____

_ you took the soft way _____ when you said, "We'll _____

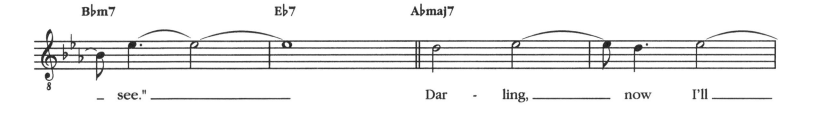

_ see." _____ Dar - ling, _____ now I'll _____

_ let you _____ do it the hard way

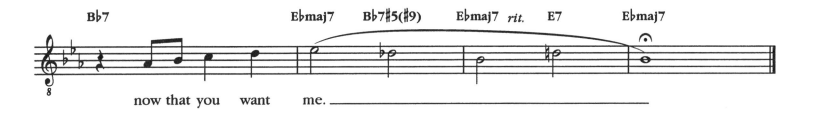

now that you want me. _____

EARLY MORNING MOOD

By CHET BAKER

Moderately

Bass Intro N.C.

26

FREEWAY

By CHET BAKER

*Harmony is implied

HAVE YOU MET MISS JONES?

from I'D RATHER BE RIGHT

Words by LORENZ HART
Music by RICHARD RODGERS

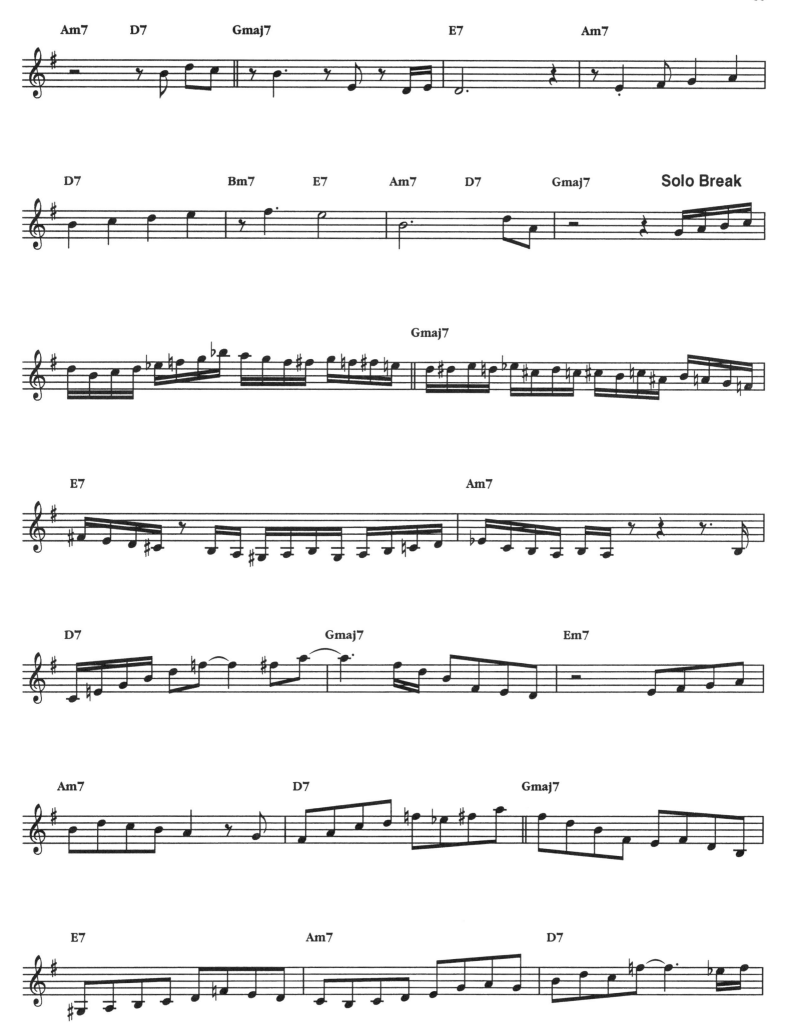

34

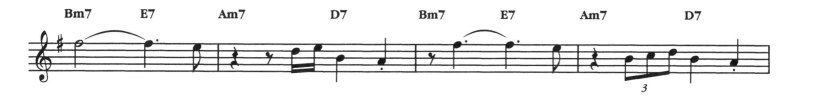

HOW HIGH THE MOON

from TWO FOR THE SHOW

Words by NANCY HAMILTON
Music by MORGAN LEWIS

39

I GET ALONG WITHOUT YOU VERY WELL

(EXCEPT SOMETIMES)

Inspired by a poem written by J.B. Thompson

Words and Music by HOAGY CARMICHAEL

LET'S GET LOST

from the Paramount Picture HAPPY GO LUCKY

Words by FRANK LOESSER
Music by JIMMY McHUGH

44

Dm7   G7   Cmaj7   F7   E7   Am7

To cel - e - brate ___ this ___ night we've found ___ each oth - er, ___

Dm7   G7   Cmaj7   A7   Dm7   G7

mmm   mmm _____ let's get lost. _____

Trumpet

Dmaj7   Abm7b5   Dmaj7   Abm7b5   Db7

F#m7   B7#5   F#m7b5   B7#5

Em7   A7   Dmaj7   Bm7

F#m7   B7   Em7

A7   Dmaj7   Abm7b5   Dmaj7

Abm7b5   Db7   F#m7   B7#5

LOADED

By BERNARD MILLER

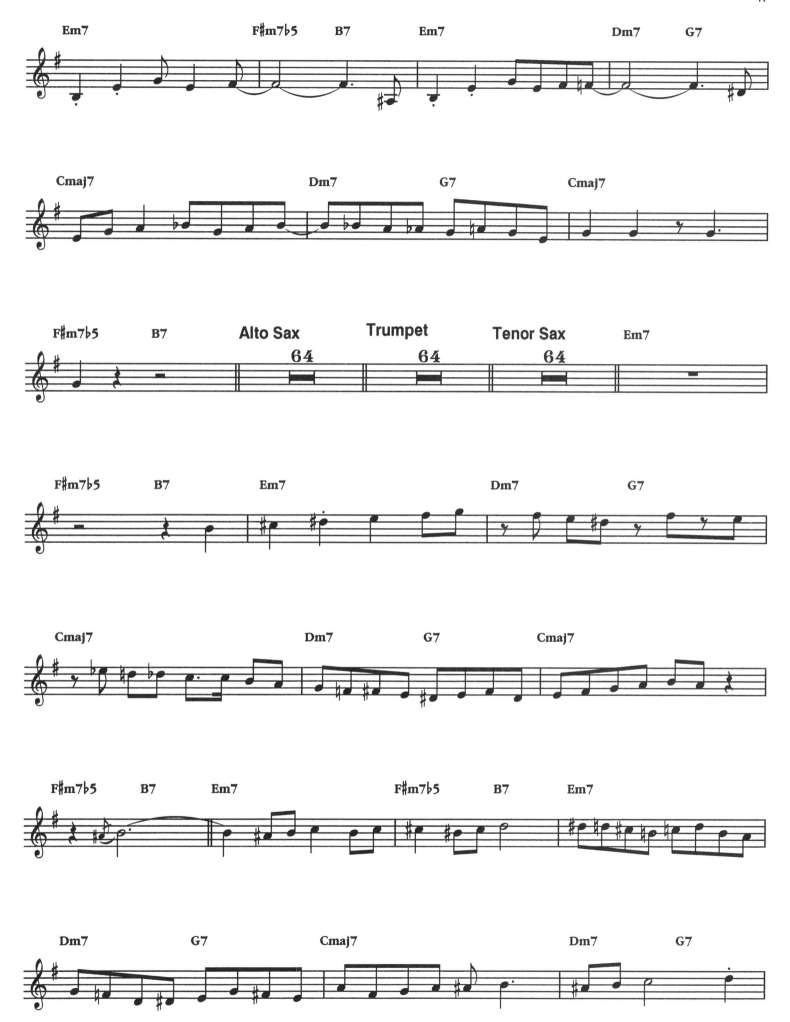

50

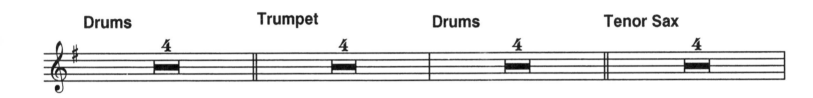

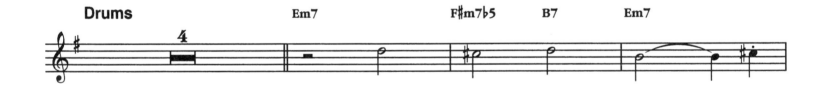

MOONLIGHT BECOMES YOU
from the Paramount Picture ROAD TO MOROCCO

Words by JOHNNY BURKE
Music by JAMES VAN HEUSEN

MY FUNNY VALENTINE

from BABES IN ARMS

Words by LORENZ HART
Music by RICHARD RODGERS

Tenor Sax

31

rubato

MY OLD FLAME
from the Paramount Picture BELLE OF THE NINETIES

Words and Music by ARTHUR JOHNSTON
and SAM COSLOW

HOW DEEP IS THE OCEAN
(HOW HIGH IS THE SKY)

Words and Music by IRVING BERLIN

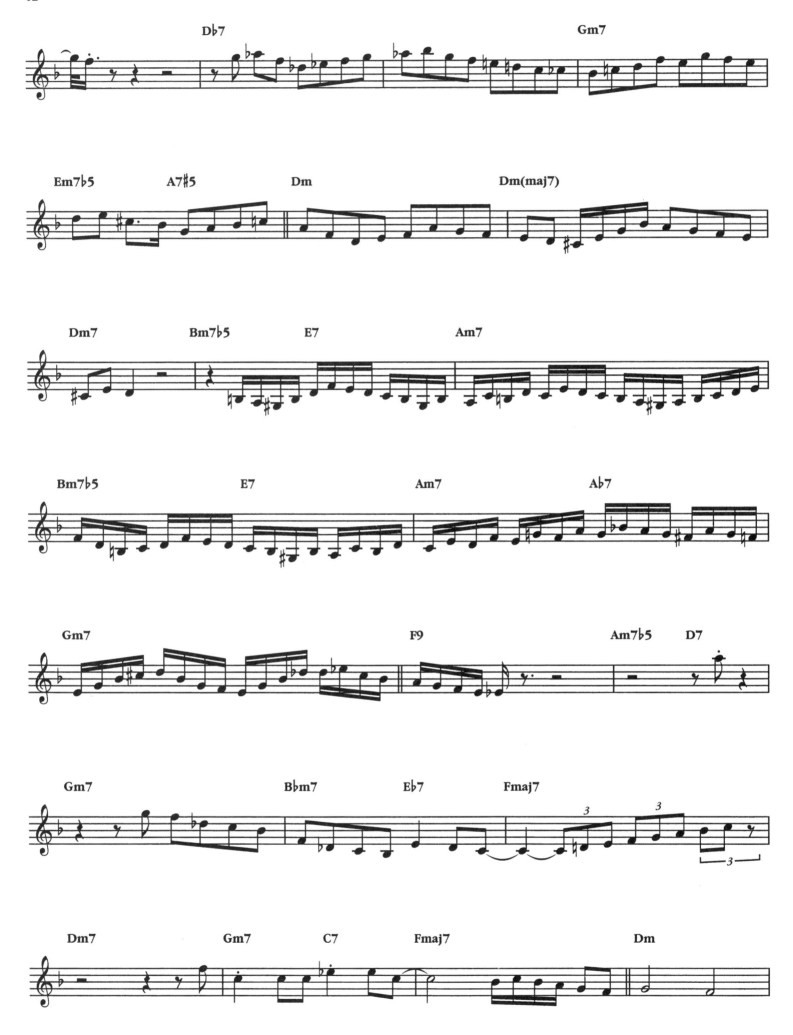

OUT OF NOWHERE

from the Paramount Picture DUDE RANCH

Words by EDWARD HEYMAN
Music by JOHNNY GREEN

69

73

SEPTEMBER SONG
from the Musical Play KNICKERBOCKER HOLIDAY

Words by MAXWELL ANDERSON
Music by KURT WEILL

Slowly

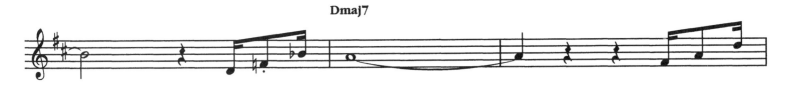

SOLAR

By MILES DAVIS

Brightly

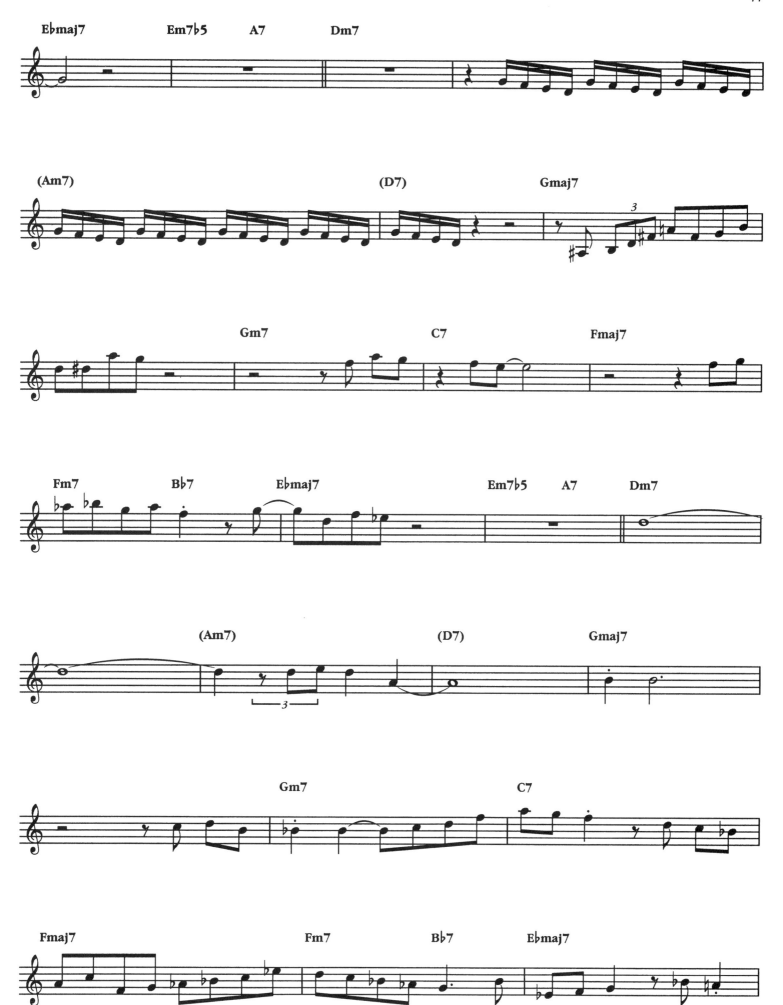

PENT UP HOUSE

By SONNY ROLLINS

STELLA BY STARLIGHT

from the Paramount Picture THE UNINVITED

Words by NED WASHINGTON
Music by VICTOR YOUNG

THE TOUCH OF YOUR LIPS

Words and Music by RAY NOBLE

92

93

TUNE UP

By MILES DAVIS

WITCH DOCTOR

By BOB COOPER

106

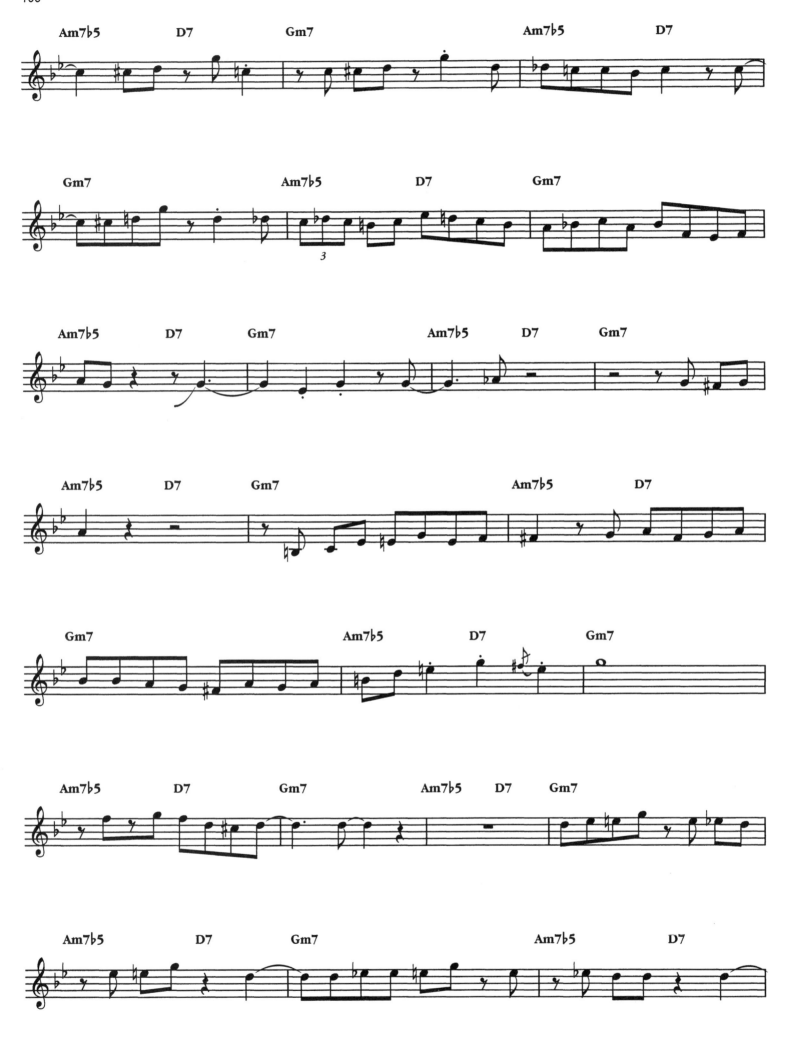

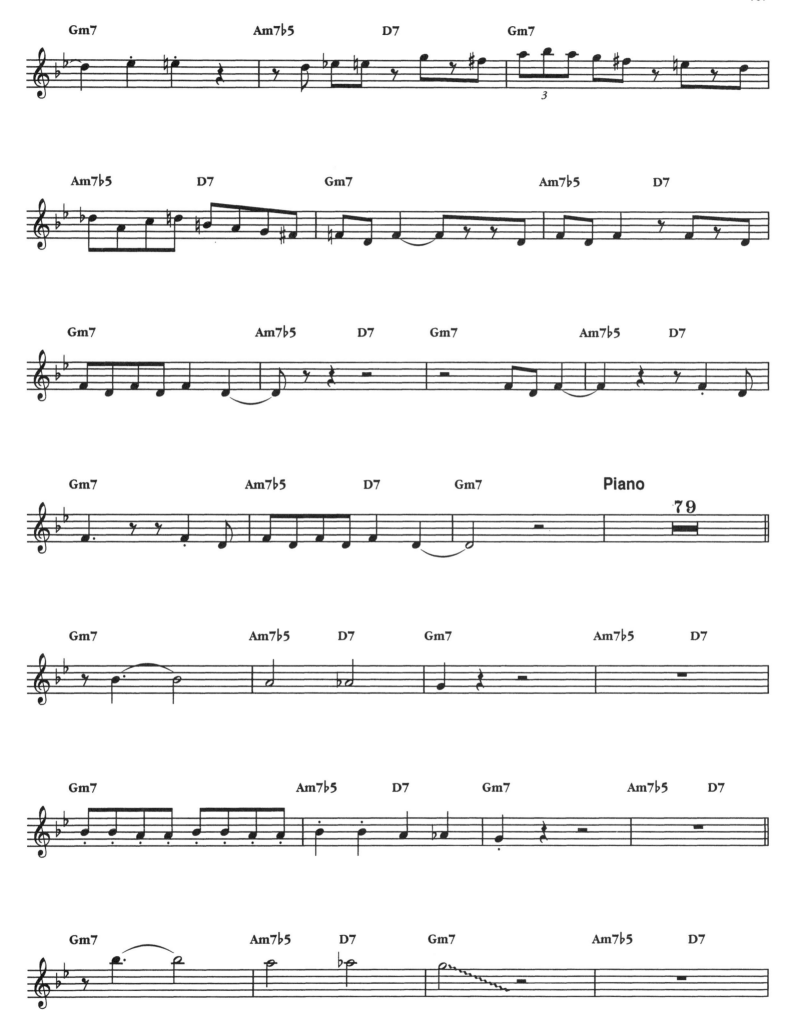

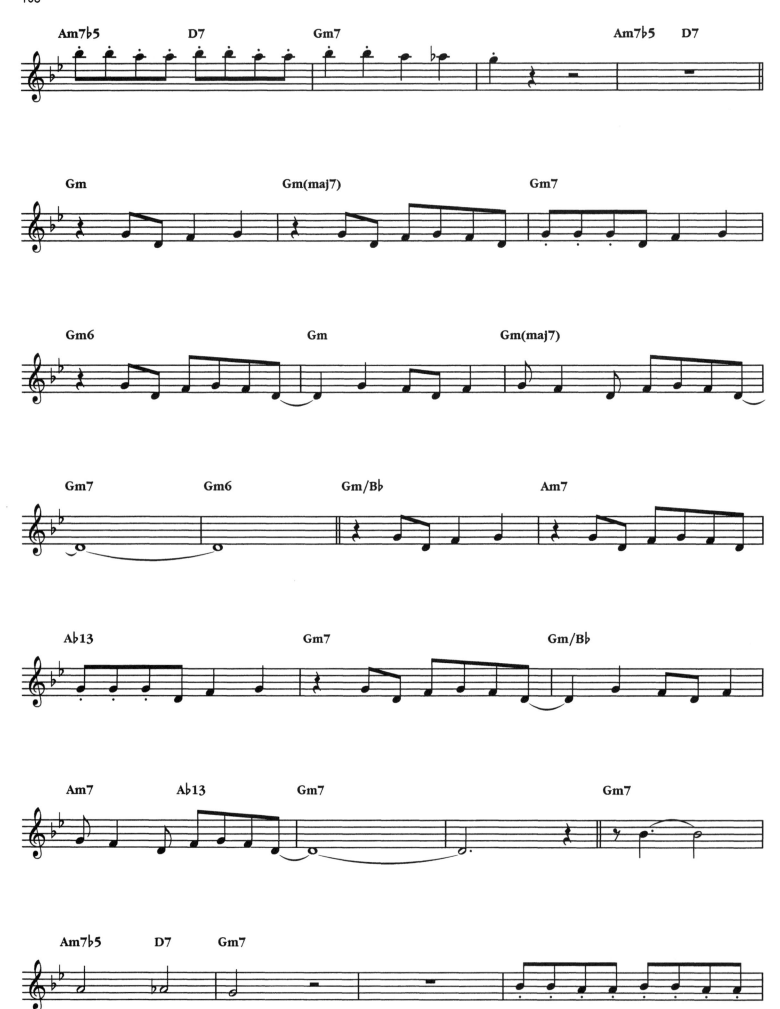

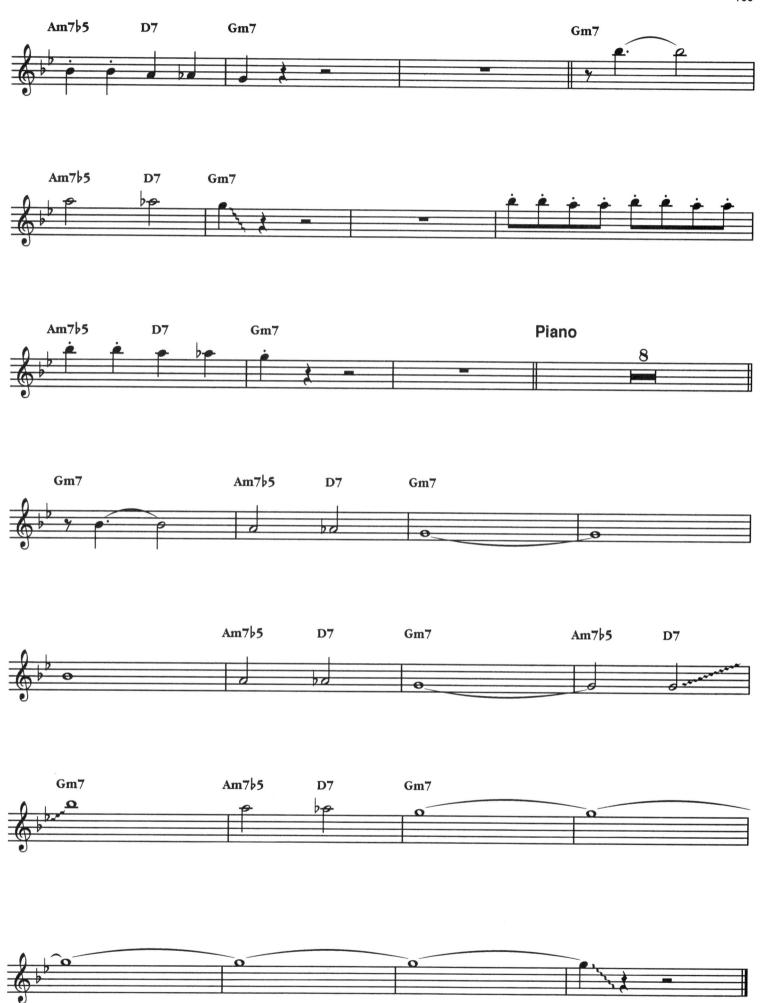

YOU BETTER GO NOW

from NEW FACES OF 1936

Words by BICKLEY REICHNER
Music by ROBERT GRAHAM

THERE WILL NEVER BE ANOTHER YOU

from the Motion Picture ICELAND

Lyric by MACK GORDON
Music by HARRY WARREN

mil - lion dreams, how can they come true, if there will __

nev - er be _____ an - oth - er you.   *(sing scat syllables)*

114

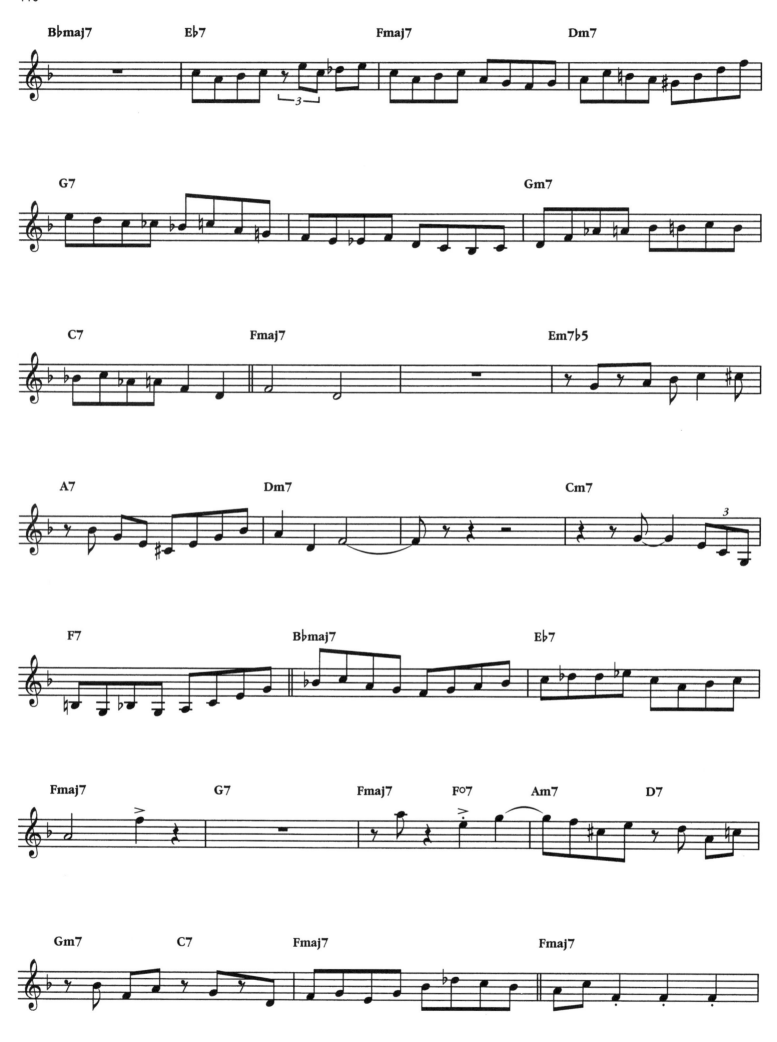

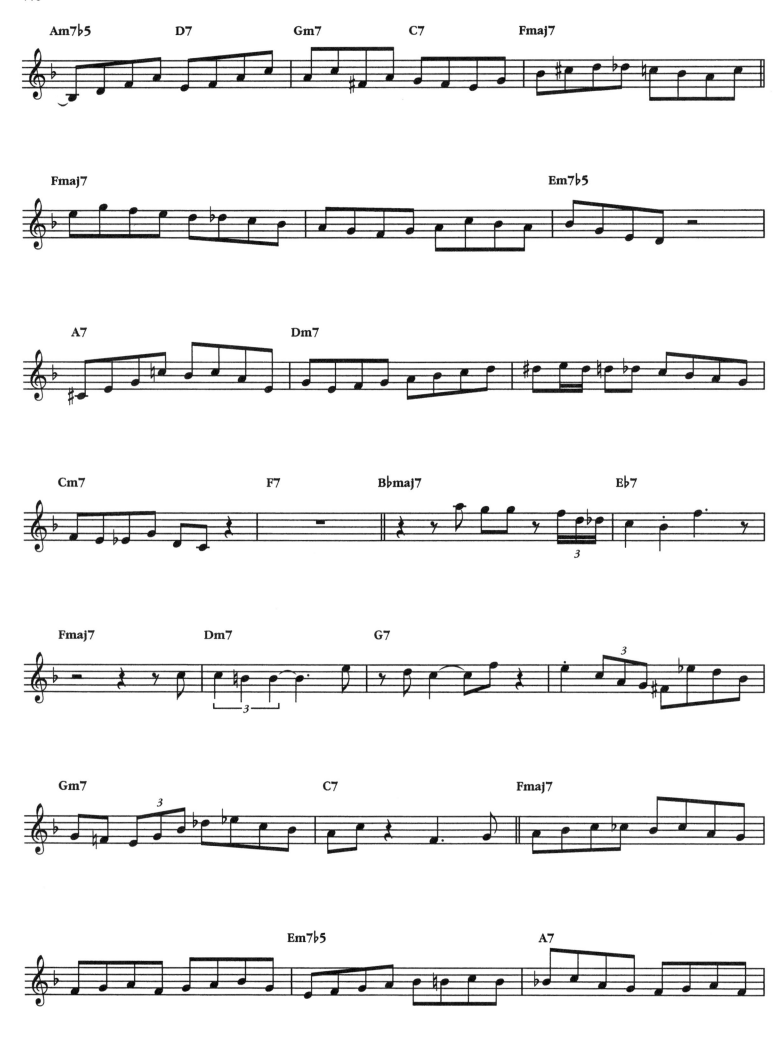

120

will be oth - er lips _____ that I _____ may _____ kiss, _

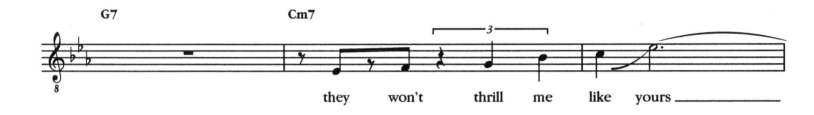

they won't thrill me like yours _____

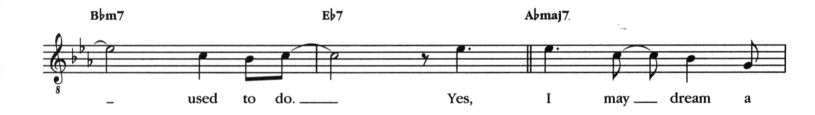

_ used to do. _____ Yes, I may _ dream a

mil - lion dreams, how can they come true, if

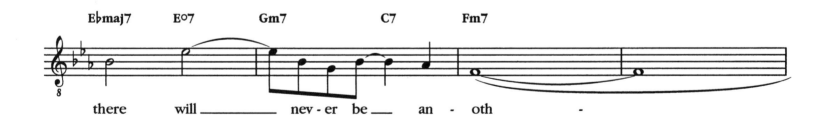

there will _____ nev - er be _ an - oth -

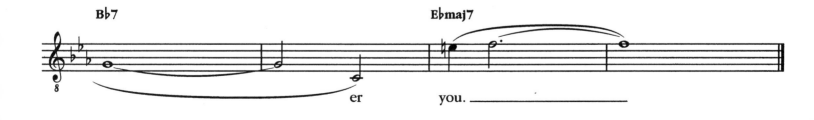

er you. _____